Disney

5-
MINUTE
GIRL
POWER
STORIES

Disney PRESS

Los Angeles • New York

Contents

Ride the Waves

It was a hot and lazy afternoon on the island of Kauai. Lilo and Stitch were at their favorite place: the beach.

Lilo took pictures. And Stitch—well, Stitch did what he did best. He caused mischief!

Lilo's older sister, Nani, was also at the beach, with David. They were checking out a poster for a surfing competition when they noticed Stitch getting into trouble.

"Guys, you can't dash all over the beach causing trouble!" said Nani when things were calm again.

"How about you two put your energy to good use?" said David. "The Kauai Kurl Surf Competition is next Saturday!"

A surfing competition? No way. That was Nani's thing, not Lilo's.

"I don't think so," said Lilo, shaking her head. Beside her, Stitch shook his own head so fast he almost fell backward.

"Come on," said Nani. "I'll teach you both how to surf like champions!" Lilo hadn't thought of it that way. If surfing meant more time with Nani and Stitch . . . Lilo would do it.

"Okay, we're in!" said Lilo.

First stop: the surf shop!

"We have to rent you a board," said Nani as they walked into the store. She studied a wall of colorful surfboards. They towered over Lilo and Stitch!

"Hey, Lilo," said Myrtle, a classmate. Lilo and Myrtle didn't always get along. "I didn't know you were a surfer."

Lilo eyed the bar of surf wax Myrtle held. "My sister is going to help me surf like a champion for the competition next weekend," Lilo said.

"I entered the competition, too . . . and *I'm* going to win!" said Myrtle.

"Don't worry, Lilo," said Nani as they left the surf shop. "Surfing isn't about winning. It's about having fun, right?" Lilo wasn't so sure. She was beginning to wonder why she had agreed to enter the competition in the first place.

"You are going to have
to get out to the waves
all by yourself,"
Nani said.

"First lie down
flat on your belly,"
she instructed.
"Now paddle with
your arms.

"Now imagine a big
wave is coming, and push
up quickly. Plant both feet
on the board at the same
time, and . . . *there*! That
was good, Lilo!"

"You're supposed to do that *in* the water, I think," boomed a big voice, followed by some laughter. It was their friend Mr. Bubbles!

"Nani is teaching us in the sand first," said Lilo. "But I think we're ready to try it out there!" Lilo pointed to the waves, and Stitch nodded.

"Okay, then," said Nani, smiling. "Remember, if you get knocked down, just get right back up again."

Lilo and Stitch picked up the surfboard and headed for the water.

But before they could even get onto their board, a wave sent them tumbling. Lilo remembered what Nani had said, and together with Stitch, she got right back up.

Lilo and Stitch paddled out. Nani followed on her own board. The whole family was together on the ocean!

Lilo and Stitch practiced hard that day, but they still couldn't stand on their board.

For the rest of the week, Lilo and Stitch focused on strength training and practicing their surfing technique.

By Friday, Lilo and Stitch were riding the waves! Lilo's body felt strong and steady.

Finally, it was the big day.

"I'm nervous," Lilo said.

"Lilo, you've practiced all week," Nani replied, "and your hard work will pay off. Just do your best. We'll show the competition what the Pelekai sisters can do!"

"And Stitch?" said Stitch.

"Yes, of course!" said Nani. "Stitch, too! Let's go!"

At the beach, they saw many of the competitors lined up with their surfboards, their eyes fixed on the waves. Lilo joined them. She was focused. She was tough. She was—

"Intimidated?" said Myrtle, interrupting Lilo's thoughts. "You should be. Get ready to wave goodbye to first place!"

But Lilo didn't let Myrtle get to her. Instead, she remembered what Nani had said. She had practiced. She was ready.

The official blew the whistle, and everyone ran to the waves.

Together, Lilo and Stitch paddled out, jumped up, and stuck the landing with all four of their feet.

Myrtle hit a wave the wrong way and totally wiped out. Instead of getting back on her board, Myrtle dragged herself to shore.

Out on the waves, Lilo and Stitch were riding high!

I'll show them what we can do, Lilo thought.

"Should we try out a trick, Stitch?" she asked.

Stitch nodded, an excited grin on his face.

CHOMP! Stitch bit the board leash. Lilo swung him around and around and around, and . . .

Oh no! Wipeout!

Fortunately, Nani was close by. She came to the rescue.

"Are you okay?" asked Nani as she pulled the friends onto her board.

"I think so, but our board is gone. We'll never win now!" Lilo moaned.

"You don't have to show off to show that you're strong," said Nani. "And the most important thing isn't winning, right? It's—"

"Getting right back up again when you get knocked down," Lilo finished.

Soon a massive wave came toward them.

"Imagine your heart and the wave's heart are one and the same," Nani said as the wave came closer. The words helped Lilo feel braver.

Lilo hopped up onto Nani's shoulders, and then Stitch scrambled up onto Lilo's shoulders. Together, they surfed all the way to shore.

Lilo, Stitch, and Nani won the award for best teamwork. The whole family—'ohana—did it together!

The special prize was a trophy and a new surfboard.

"For me?" Lilo said as the judge handed her the sweet board.

"For you, Sister," said Nani, nodding. "You deserve it. And now we can keep practicing . . . for next year's surfing competition!"

Officer McDimples on Duty

Woody, Bo, and their friends moved from town to town with a carnival, helping kids and toys along the way. As the carnival set up in a new place, the toys made their way to a nearby playground for some fun.

A boy raced Duke Caboom down the slide while Officer Giggle McDimples, Woody, Bo, and her sheep took a ride on the merry-go-round.

Amid all the fun, Bo and Giggle noticed a sad taco toy in the sand beside them. When the merry-go-round slowed, Bo whispered into Giggle's ear, "Once the area is clear, we investigate the taco."

As soon as the kids left the playground, Ducky and Bunny got up.

"That was awful," groaned Taco.

"You mean awesome," said Bunny. "Right?"

"Awful," repeated Taco.

Giggle approached the toy. "Officer McDimples at your service. What seems to be the trouble, sir?"

"I don't know," said Taco with a sigh. "Playing with kids is . . . boring." All the toys gasped.

Giggle held up her hand, quieting them. "Sounds like you're in need of a little detective work." She collected Taco's information and then asked if he remembered ever having fun at a playground.

Taco smiled as he recalled a sunny day. "The grass was green, the sky was blue, and a kid grabbed me, chewed me a few times, and chucked me into the grass. It was awesome!"

"This is a case of mistaken identity," said Giggle. "Taco, you are not meant to play with kids. You're a pet toy!"

Suddenly, Taco was very excited. Giggle was, too. As the head of the Pet Patrol, pets were her specialty.

"So what kind of pet toy is he?" asked Woody.

"We are about to find out, Sheriff," said Giggle with a grin.

The toys watched as Giggle got to work trying to determine the right pet for Taco. "We have several suspects here," said Giggle. "Dog, cat, parakeet, rabbit, hamster, horse. Any one of these pets could be our target."

After a few moments, she turned toward Woody. "We'll need to run a squeaker-detection test," said Giggle.

Woody threw his lasso around Taco, and at Giggle's command, all the toys worked together to pull it tight.

SQUEEEEAAAAK!

The jubilant sound made Taco laugh and laugh.

"As I suspected," said Giggle. "You're a dog toy."

Bo led everyone to a large map posted outside the playground. Giggle narrowed her eyes. "It's a dangerous mission, but this task force can handle it. Let's go!"

"Where are we going?" asked Taco.

"Dog park," said Giggle.

Just as they were about to discuss transportation, a woman approached with her dogs. The toys dropped to the ground.

"Now where is the dog park?" she muttered, looking up at the map.

The toys watched, hopeful, as the dogs checked out Taco—but neither of them seemed interested.

As the woman turned to leave, Bo and Woody quickly helped all the toys into the bottom of her dog stroller. They remained hidden as she unknowingly pushed them to the dog park.

When they arrived, the toys crept behind a patch of shrubs and watched the dogs running, sniffing, and playing inside the park.

Taco wanted to race through the gates, but Giggle held up her hand. "It's my sworn duty as an officer of the law to make sure this is done correctly." Bo launched Giggle into the dog park.

Giggle's eyes landed on a young pup wagging her tail. She knew she had found the one for Taco.

Giggle rolled off a dog's head and used a leaf as cover to make her way back to the other toys.

"White and tan, long tail. Southeast corner," announced Giggle.

"Yes!" Taco cheered.

"How do we get him there?" asked Woody.

They quickly got into position and waited for the perfect moment. "Now!" Giggle said. Bo ran a few steps, dropped Taco, and kicked him with all her might. Taco soared over the gate and into the park.

The dog spotted Taco and began wagging her long tail. She leaped into the air and caught him in her mouth! Then she chewed on him as she ran, squeaking him all the way.

"What do you have there, Gigi?" said a young girl. "A taco! How cool!"

"Another Pet Patrol case closed," said Giggle with pride.

"And another happy toy," added Bo.

The toys watched as the girl and her dog continued having a blast, throwing and fetching Taco. They knew he was enjoying every chasing, chewing, squeaking second—and that made them feel happy, too.

The Tambourine Dance

Ariel loved the market. There was always something new to see.

One day she saw dancers.

"This is our traditional tambourine dance," one of the girls announced. "Come learn how to do it! I'll be teaching a class tomorrow. Bring a tambourine!"

Ariel told Scuttle about it later.

"I'm going to my first dance class," she said. "I want to be like the girls at the market. They had something called a tambourine. It made the loveliest sound. Do you know where I can get one?"

"A tambourine is a kind of fruit," said Scuttle. "You could find one at the fruit seller."

"Thanks, Scuttle! You know everything!" Ariel said.

Later that day, Ariel went straight to the fruit seller.

"One tambourine, please," she said.

"No tambourines here. Try the music store."

Ariel walked across the street and found something that looked like what the girls in the market had.

"It sounds like shells clinking together in the ocean," she said to the shopkeeper. Ariel purchased the instrument and ran to show Scuttle.

"Scuttle!" Ariel called. "*This* is a tambourine."

"Of course! That's what I meant," he said.

"The girls danced like this," said Ariel. She held the tambourine up high in one hand, did a few steps, and started to spin until . . . *crash!*

"Not bad for a first try," said Scuttle.

Ariel frowned and tried again.

The next day, Ariel was nervous as she approached the class. Even though she had tried to practice, dancing was difficult for her.

"Welcome," said the teacher. "I'm Isabella. Thanks for coming. This dance is a bit tricky to learn, but remember, everyone here started out as a beginner, just like you."

Except they've had legs forever, Ariel thought.

"Okay, class, let's begin!" said Isabella.

Ariel stepped in line, but she stumbled and nearly fell on every spin. She couldn't remember which was her right leg and which was her left.

After class, Ariel met her friends at the dock. "How was dancing?" asked Sebastian.

"I'm hopeless," Ariel said. "I wish it was easy, like singing. I'm no good at spinning."

"When you were young, singing was hard for you, too," said Sebastian. "But you got better and better after you practiced."

"You've always wanted to try dancing," said Flounder. "You can't give up now!"

"I have an idea!" said Scuttle. "We'll help you practice at the beach."

Down near the shore, Sebastian spoke first. "I can teach you tricks for remembering left and right that I learned from conducting the orchestra."

Flounder joined in. "I'm great at spinning underwater, so I can help with the turns."

"And I'll squawk encouragements!" Scuttle finished.

"Okay," said Ariel. "With all your help, I'll have to get better."

Sebastian started by showing Ariel how to remember her left and right.

Then she practiced switching between her left and right leg, and she got better.

After a bit, Scuttle squawked, "You've got it, kid!"

Next she practiced with Flounder.

"Before I spin underwater, I always find something straight ahead to look at," Flounder said. "That way, after I spin around, I'll know when to stop."

Ariel spun around and stopped when she saw Flounder again.

"A little wobbly, but much better!" said Flounder.

"A spinning sensation!" squawked Scuttle.

At her next dance class, Ariel had much more fun. Then she asked about the ribbons the other dancers had on their tambourines.

"They were gifts from our families for our first performance," one of the dancers said. "It's tradition."

Ariel wondered whether her family could possibly know about this tradition. Plus, how would her sisters find ribbons in the sea?

After class, Ariel found Flounder, Sebastian, and Scuttle and told them about the ribbon tradition. A smile lit Flounder's face. He had a plan!

Ariel spent every free moment practicing. All her hard work was paying off. She was becoming a good dancer!

On the day of the performance, Flounder had arranged a surprise.
One by one, King Triton and each of Ariel's sisters presented her with
special seaweed ribbons. Eric gave her a satin ribbon, too.

Ariel was thrilled to be a part of the tradition. "I couldn't have done
it without you," she told her friends.

"Of course you could have," said Sebastian. "You're a natural!"

"You'll do great!" said Flounder.

"You're tambourine terrific!" said Scuttle.

Finally, it was time for the class
to perform. Ariel's whole family
came to watch!

The girls twirled and danced while the tambourines jingled. After the final spin, the crowd cheered.

After the performance, a little girl said to Ariel, "You did a great job in the dance. I wish I could dance like that, but it looked so hard."

Ariel handed the girl her tambourine. "Go on, shake it," she said. "That was the only thing I could do when I started. I couldn't spin, and I didn't know my right from my left. It took a lot of practice, but if I can do it, so can you. Go on, give it a try!"

A Day with Moana

The morning sun rose high over Motunui as Moana headed through the village.

"Good morning!" Moana said, approaching two women with baskets of food. "How are things?"

"Hi, Moana! It's a fine day. But we're low on sugarcane and won't have enough for what we're making."

"I can help!" Moana volunteered. "I'll gather some more for you."

"Can we come, too?" a girl named Fetuao asked Moana. "We love exploring."

"Yes, but we all have to stick together. The island is big, and I don't want anyone to get lost. But if something does happen, just stay where you are and wait for me to come find you," Moana said.

"We promise," the children said. They were so excited to spend the day with Moana.

Moana and the children set off toward the forest.

"I love sugarcane," a girl named Masina said. Moana and the children talked about how many things they used sugarcane for.

"I like to just eat it by itself," a boy named Toa said.

The forest was full of giant trees, colorful plants, and rocks and boulders of all sizes. Without any clear paths to walk along, it was obvious why Moana had told them to stick together. Moana looked for visual signs to help her find her way.

"See, that rock over there looks a little like Pua!" Moana said. The kids loved Pua and could picture him as if he were right there.

Moana pulled aside some thick green vines, revealing a large grove of
coconut trees.

"Can we stop for a snack?" Laumei asked.

"That's just what I was thinking," Moana replied. Laumei and Toa
scrambled up a tree. They picked the ripest fruits, then tossed them down.

After they broke open the coconuts against a rock, they devoured the
white meat and drank the sweet water inside. It was a refreshing break.

"Do we have time for a game?" Fetuao asked.

Since they'd reached the coconut grove sooner than Moana had expected, she figured a quick game wouldn't hurt. "How about a round of hide-and-seek?" she asked.

"Yes!" the children exclaimed. They scattered in every direction.

"But stay close by!" Moana called after them. She shut her eyes and began to count.

While he was looking for a place to hide, Toa saw a colorful bird he'd never seen before. He began to follow the bird.

"Time's up!" Moana yelled. She opened her eyes and began to look for the children.

In a matter of minutes, Moana had found Fetuao, Laumei, and Masina. That meant only Toa was left, but no matter where she looked, Moana couldn't find him.

"Good job, Toa! You found the best hiding spot. You can come out now!" Moana said. When he didn't appear, Moana was worried he was lost.

Meanwhile, Toa had followed the colorful bird all the way back to its nest. He turned around to show his friends, but realized he was all alone. He started to worry, but he remembered what Moana had said earlier, and he sat down and waited for her to find him.

Moana and the other children went back through the vines toward the Pua-shaped rock. It was there that Moana noticed some bright blue feathers.

"Maybe he went up this way," she said.

They picked up the feathers and continued
walking. Not far away, they came upon another
clearing . . . and there was someone familiar sitting on
a rock.

"Toa!" Fetuao cried as Moana hugged him.
They were relieved to see he was safe and sound.

"I'm sorry," he said. "I didn't mean to go off so far! I was following that bird, and it ended up here." He pointed to a nest in a tree hollow. Moana looked up to see a bird with several baby chicks. Toa had stumbled upon a mother bird as she was returning to her family!

"Well, it looks like everyone is back together again," Moana said, smiling.

"Look over there!" directed Fetuao.

"That's the tallest grass I've ever seen!" added Masina.

Moana followed the girls and couldn't believe her eyes. Thanks to their unexpected detour, they had found a shortcut to the sugarcane field!

"This is exactly what we're looking for!" Moana cheered. She broke off pieces of the sugarcane stalks and passed them to the children, who arranged them in piles. After gathering as much as their arms could carry, it was time to head home.

"Before we go," Moana said, "let's create a sign to mark this new shortcut."

They carved an outline of the bird into the ground with sticks. Finally, they stuck the blue feathers they'd collected in the ground next to their new landmark.

It was a perfect way to end their afternoon.

Soon Moana and the children arrived
back in the village. Moana gave the basket
of sugarcane to the women, who were
delighted to see the bright, juicy stalks.

"Thank you, Moana!" one woman exclaimed.
"These are wonderful."

"It was our pleasure," Moana replied.

As they said goodbye, Moana gave each child a *hongi*, pressing her nose against theirs.

"When I grow up, I want to be just like you," Toa said.

Moana was touched. "As Gramma Tala says, you can be whatever your heart tells you."

Moana smiled all the way home. Her heart felt as full as the basket of sugarcane.

THE
LION KING

Nala's Great Adventure

Nala was sitting at the edge of Pride Rock, gazing out at the land, when she had an idea. "Hey, Simba!" Nala called. "Want to go on an adventure?"

"What kind of adventure?" Simba asked. "Is today the day we find our perfect clubhouse?"

"You mean our cub-house?" Nala chuckled. "That sounds like the perfect adventure. We'll find a place to hang out where we can do whatever we want!"

Nala turned to her mother. "Can we go?"

"Yes, Nala," she said. "But you and Simba must be home before dark."

"And wait for Zazu!" Sarabi said, having overheard them.

"Sure, Mom!" Simba shouted as he ran away. Turning to Nala, he added, whispering, "Sure . . . if Zazu can catch us. Come on! Follow me!"

Simba was taking Nala to a new hiding place he had found that he thought could be perfect for their cub-house. He couldn't wait to see what she thought of it!

"Isn't this the best hideout?" Simba said as he leaped up on a large rock. "We can do whatever we want and make it our own."

"It's cool," Nala replied, "but doesn't someone else live here?"

Just then, Scar walked around the corner. "Ah, my favorite nephew," Scar grumbled.

"Uncle Scar, I'm your *only* nephew," Simba said, laughing. "Look! I brought my friend Nala!"

Scar did not seem pleased. "What are you two doing here?" he asked.

"We're looking for our very own cub-house," Simba explained. "Come on, Nala! I'll show you the dark part of the cave."

Scar scowled. He did *not* want them hanging around his home.

"Well, if you must," Scar began, already plotting how to get rid of Simba. "But did I mention that Zazu is coming for a visit soon? He checks up on me, you know. . . ."

"We were kinda trying to avoid Zazu," Simba said.

"Time to go check out another cub-house option, I guess," Nala told Simba.

"I think you're right! Bye, Uncle Scar!" Simba called.

The pair ran off before Zazu could catch up to them.

"Where should we go now?" Simba asked.

Nala thought for a minute. "I know!" she said at last. "We can go to the water hole! Nobody, especially not Zazu, will find us there."

There were always lots of animals gathered at the water hole. Lost in the crowd, the two friends would be able to do whatever they wanted!

"Check it out!" Nala exclaimed as she jumped and splashed in the water.

"Hey, you got me wet!" Simba yelled.

But it was so much fun that he soon jumped in, too! The two cubs ran and played together. This spot seemed perfect for their cub-house.

The fun and games continued . . . until Simba bumped right into an elephant's leg!

"Whoa! Watch out!" Nala said. They were soon surrounded by a parade of elephants, none of whom seemed to notice the two lion cubs running among them!

"Nala, look out!" Simba cried. A crash of rhinoceroses was rushing toward the water, and Nala was in their path!

"Run!" Simba shouted. He raced over and pushed Nala aside just in time.

As Simba raced away from the rhinoceroses, he ran right into a colony of flamingos!

"Sorry!" he hollered as he scrambled away.

"I think I'm ready to leave now," Simba said as he gasped for air.

"Me too," Nala added. "I'm not sure this was the place for our cub-house."

The tired cubs started out across the savannah, but then Nala had another idea. "Follow me!" she said to Simba.

Nala led Simba straight to the base of Rafiki's tree.

"Now this is what I call a perfect cub-house," Simba said as he began to climb up into the tree.

"It's so nice," Nala replied as she followed him. "I'm gonna find my own branch."

The two friends were so exhausted from their adventures that they settled down to nap for a while.

"What are you doing?" Rafiki asked, waking the two cubs abruptly.

Nala looked up groggily. "Wha—?"

"You don't belong here!" Rafiki said. He scratched his chin and muttered, "You belong up there!"

He pointed toward Pride Rock.

The cubs looked toward their home. They spotted their mothers looking for them.

"We were supposed to be home before dark," Nala said, "and I *am* kinda getting hungry."

"Me too," Simba added wistfully.

The cubs thanked Rafiki and then headed back toward Pride Rock.

"There you are!" Zazu called from above as they got closer. "Where have you been all day?"

"Sorry, Zazu," Nala said. "We were just looking for a cub-house."

"A cub-what?" asked Zazu.

"A cub-house," Nala explained. "Scar didn't want us around—"

"Then we almost got crushed at the water hole," Simba added, "and, well—"

"We haven't found it yet . . . but we will!" Nala said. "For now, we're ready to go home."

Settling in at Pride Rock, the cubs cuddled up with their mothers in their warm, cozy cave.

"I still want to find a cub-house someday," Nala said, "but for now it's good to be home."

Disney

MULAN

Honor for Father

It was nearly time for the Tournament of the Imperial Courts—and Mulan's father's birthday. Mulan dreamed of winning the prized scroll; it would make the perfect gift!

"Father, do you think I will win?" she asked Fa Zhou.

"Mulan, the correct question is, will you honor our family by doing your best?"

He smiled, and Mulan smiled back. But another question bothered her: what if she did not?

Early the next morning, Mulan practiced with her friends.
"Hold still, Mushu," Mulan said, aiming her arrow.
"Can we fight, too?" Mushu asked. "Cri-Kee says he can
take down the others with one flick of his feeler."

"Thanks, guys. But I have to do this on my own," Mulan said. "The other warriors will be bigger than me. Stronger, too. If I'm going to win, I'll need to outsmart them."

"Just stay alive," Mushu said, smiling. "I'll see you at showtime."

Finally, it was time to start. As the crowd gathered,
Mulan caught a glimpse of her family in the stands.
Her father gave her a nod.
Mulan remembered his advice: do your very best.

The master of ceremonies welcomed everyone and explained the rules.

"Each warrior will battle one opponent at a time. The winner advances to the next round. All matches must take place within the circle. Stepping out of bounds results in disqualification."

Archery was the first event. Upon hearing Mulan's name, Mushu led the Fa family cheering squad in a rousing chant.

The crowd burst into applause.

Then the master of ceremonies announced Mulan's competitor.
"Sou Mai Ti!"

Mulan frowned. Sou Mai Ti was intimidating.

Just then, the gong rang. The competitors sent apples into the air
using their kickstands.

Sou Mai Ti was good . . . but Mulan used a bit more creativity.

Rather than aiming for a straight line, Mulan made a smiley face on the target board!

Fortunately, her cleverness was rewarded!

"Fa Mulan wins!" announced the master of ceremonies.

Mulan's father nodded with approval. *Maybe this will be Father's best birthday yet,* she thought.

Next, Mulan battled with staffs against Pao Er Fu.

Mushu rallied the crowd with another cheer. But in all the excitement, he almost fell into the circle. The crowd gasped.

Mulan hesitated, and Pao seized his opportunity.

Pao threw his staff directly at Mulan! She quickly ducked, turned, and split Pao's weapon in half.

The crowd oohed. Mulan had won!

That was close, she thought. Mulan could not let Mushu break her concentration again.

Battle after battle,
Mulan defeated every
warrior who came her way.
The scroll was almost hers.

"We are down to the last two warriors," called the master of ceremonies. "Fa Mulan and Wan Na Pu!"

Mulan gulped as Wan entered the circle. He was the fiercest competitor of all.

For the final round, the warriors chose their weapons. Wan revealed two tridents!

Mulan took a deep breath, then brandished the sword of Shan-Yu.

Bong! The gong rang out, and the battle began.

Mulan quickly realized that, on the ground, Wan's size and skill overshadowed hers. But balance was her advantage.

So she jumped up onto a pole. From there, she matched his every move.

As the fighting intensified, so did Mushu's cheer.

Mulan's friends formed a tower with Mushu on top. The noise from the crowd swelled.

Mulan raised her sword. *Father's birthday will be perfect!* she thought.

But then everything went wrong.

Mushu lost his balance, sending him, Little Brother, and Cri-Kee flying toward the ring. To make matters worse, Wan's trident was headed right for them!

"Mulan, help!" cried Mushu.

All thoughts of winning left Mulan's mind. She had to save her friends! Mulan chopped down a beam and hoped it would block the trident.

It worked! Wan's trident hit the pole instead of the animals.

But in all the excitement, Mulan made a big mistake.

"Fa Mulan has stepped outside the circle. She is disqualified. Wan Na Pu wins!" the master of ceremonies announced.

After the tournament, Mulan sat with her father once more.
"Defeat was not the gift I wanted to give you for your birthday.
I lost the tournament and our family's honor," she said sadly.

"This is not true," Fa Zhou said. "Mulan, you are brave and smart. And most important, you saved your friends today. This is the behavior of a true Fa warrior. I am honored to be your father."

He picked a blossom and placed it in Mulan's hair. "I do not need a scroll for my birthday. *You* are my greatest gift."

An Amazing Team

Aurora loved being a princess. But after spending so many years in
a quiet cottage, her life at the castle was often a bit overwhelming.

One day, Aurora was embellishing a flag for the upcoming joust. The whole kingdom gathered at this exciting event to watch knights compete on horseback.

But Aurora noticed Samson—Phillip's horse—was refusing to follow the stable hand into his stall.

"The prince is traveling, so the horse won't get to compete in the joust," the stable hand said.

"It seems like we both could use some fresh air," Aurora said to Samson. "I'd like to take you somewhere special."

But it was an awkward ride into town. Samson and
Aurora had trouble finding a rhythm. Eventually, they
reached the village. It was bustling.

Just then, Aurora had an idea.

"What if we compete in the joust together?" she whispered to Samson.

Samson was overjoyed! He immediately raced to the
field where he and Phillip used to practice.

"You are amazing!" Aurora exclaimed. "Is this where I'm going to learn how to joust?" Samson whinnied in reply.

In the joust, Aurora would have to thread a series of rings onto her lance, gallop down a straightaway, and disarm the knight pitted against her.

On the night before the tournament, Aurora revealed her plan to her parents. "Since Phillip won't be present for the joust tomorrow, I'd like to compete in his place."

After a brief silence, her mother spoke. "You're a new kind of princess," she said. "It would be our honor to have you participate."

The sun rose early the next morning. The townspeople gathered around the jousting arena, excitedly waving flags and banners. Aurora and Samson took their place among the competitors. Their hearts raced as they surveyed the scene.

"No matter what happens," Aurora whispered to Samson, "we are a team."

All of a sudden, their names were announced. It was time to compete.
Samson took off. Aurora lifted her lance and put it through all the
rings on their path!

Aurora and Samson charged toward their opponent, the valiant Sir Kaspar from the kingdom of Blumenfeld.

Now Aurora needed to disarm Sir Kaspar. But their weapons kept getting locked. She had to try a different tactic.

While Aurora was thinking of a new plan, Sir Kaspar sent her lance flying through the air!

With their weapon gone, Aurora and Samson were defeated.

At the end of the day, the winners were announced. Aurora and Samson ended up in fourth place!

"Not bad for our first tournament," Aurora said with a wink. She and Samson made an amazing team!

The Princess Polo Games

Early one morning, Jasmine flew to Kamali Field. She had been chosen as a team captain in the Princess Polo Club and was going to meet her team and the other captains! She really wanted to win the Princess Polo Club's golden trophy, just as her mother had many years earlier.

"Welcome, captains!" the chairwoman of the club said when everyone arrived. "Today you will meet your teams. Train them well. At the end of the season, a final match will determine who wins the golden trophy."

The chairwoman announced each team: the Super Sultans, the Majestic Monarchs, the Awesome Aces, and the Royal Raiders.

Jasmine couldn't wait to meet her team: the Royal Raiders!

Another team captain, Princess Farah, made fun of them. "More like the Royal *Afraiders*," Farah said to Jasmine.

Jasmine ignored her at first . . . but then she noticed Crystal wouldn't let go of her horse's neck, Amira's nose was in her book, and Zina was doing a handstand.

Jasmine went to the chairwoman and said, "There has to be some mistake."

The chairwoman shook her head. "Teams were chosen specifically for each captain's skills. You can do this, Princess Jasmine."

When Jasmine returned home, she was not very happy.

"How did your first practice go?" asked the Sultan that night.

"Not very well," Jasmine said. "I'm never going to win that trophy."

"Just do your best," said her father encouragingly.

Jasmine hoped her best would be good enough.

The next day, Jasmine taught her team how to play polo. She showed them how to hit the ball into the goal and how to stop the other team by bumping their horses or hooking their mallets.

The following day, Jasmine had an idea for practice. To help find their strengths, she set up a series of games.

Jasmine saw that once Zina realized her horse was as energetic as she was, they made a great team. They always got to the ball first!

Crystal was so stubborn about staying on her horse that she could bump into the other players to stop them from scoring.

Amira was an amazing hitter—if she pretended she was a hero from one of her books.

Jasmine used her teammates' strengths to win some games. Soon they made it to the finals to play against Farah's team: the Majestic Monarchs.

"Well, if it isn't the scaredy-cat, the bookworm, and the jumping bean," said Farah. "Get ready to lose!"

Jasmine huddled with her team moments before the first chukker, or game period. "Farah doesn't know that the very things she's teasing you for are the things that make you special. Now let's go out there and have fun!"

The game began. Zina beat Farah to the ball! The Royal Raiders got the first possession.

In the second chukker, Crystal stopped Farah from scoring three times!

Amira scored two goals all by herself in the third chukker. One of them was from all the way across the field.

After the fourth chukker, the captains rallied their teams.

"You're doing a great job!" exclaimed Jasmine. "The score is tied. We can win this!"

But the Majestic Monarchs weren't excited. Farah never passed the ball.

In the last chukker, Farah scored, and her team was up by one.

Jasmine prepared to race down the field to score another goal.
But then she saw the Majestic Monarch players and had an idea. She
called a time-out to talk to her team. Jasmine wanted to give the other
girls a chance to play and have fun.

When the Royal Raiders returned to the field, Jasmine passed the ball—straight to one of the Monarch players! Crystal and Amira blocked Farah from intercepting a pass, and Zina cheered the Monarchs all the way down the field.

In the last chukker, each Monarchs player scored a goal!

The game was over. The Monarchs had won.

Jasmine was glad that everyone on both teams had a chance to play and have fun. That was more important than winning.

"Congratulations to the Monarchs," said the chairwoman. "The medals go to the winners. But the golden trophy belongs to the most honorable player. This year, it goes to . . ."

"Princess Jasmine! You are a true leader," said the chairwoman, "just like your mother."

Jasmine gasped. "You knew my mother?"

The chairwoman smiled. "Your mother was my team captain."

Jasmine's friends and family all cheered. She had won the trophy after all!

Big Trouble in Little Rodentia

Ever since she was a little rabbit in The Burrows, Judy Hopps had dreamed of becoming the first-ever bunny cop in the Zootopia Police Department.

After lots of hard work, she graduated from the ZPD Police Academy at the top of her class. And today was her first day on the job!

She couldn't wait for her first assignment . . .

. . . which turned out to be issuing parking tickets.

Judy's ears fell in disappointment. She wanted to solve crimes, not be a meter maid.

Still, she worked hard because she wanted to do a good job. Her sharp hearing alerted her to expired meters, and she gave out 201 parking tickets—before lunchtime!

Someday, she hoped, she'd get a chance to do more.

The next day, Judy was sitting in her meter car when she heard a cry for help.

"My shop! It was just robbed! Look, he's getting away!" a local merchant shouted. "Are you a cop or not?"

"Yes! Yes! Don't worry, sir! I've got this," Judy said.

She leaped into action and ran after the criminal! "Stop! Stop in the name of the law!" she yelled at him as she chased him through an alleyway.

"Catch me if you can, cottontail!" he hollered back.

Other cops soon joined her in the chase, but Judy ran ahead. This was her big chance to fight crime!

"I got dibs!" she hollered. "Officer Hopps! I am in pursuit!"

The thief, Duke Weaselton, tried to escape among the animals in Savannah Central.

But as a rabbit, Judy knew how to make super-quick moves around big objects. She stayed on the weasel's tail!

He tried to disappear into Little Rodentia, a neighborhood of small rodents, but Judy quickly followed him.

"You! Freeze!" she said, sliding through the town's tiny entrance.

"Hey, meter maid!" one of the cops called after her. "Wait for the real cops."

But the other cops were too big to follow! Judy was the only one small enough to continue the chase.

When Duke realized that Judy was getting closer, he sped up, which caused lots of problems for the local residents—especially riders on the uptown bus!

Fortunately, Judy arrived in time to save the day!

As Judy caught up to him, he raced even faster to try to escape. Duke climbed on top of a row of Little Rodentia buildings and knocked them over . . . just like a set of dominoes.

Ka-thunk, thunk, thunk, thunk!

Judy put the buildings upright again, stopping just long enough to make sure all the rodents were safe. Then she took off after Duke again! "Hey! Stop right there!" she said, racing down the street.

Finally, Judy caught up with Duke and grabbed him.
As they struggled, Judy flung Duke across the street.
She tried to arrest him peacefully, but the weasel had
other ideas.

"Here, have a donut, copper!" Duke said with a nasty laugh.

Desperate to escape, the weasel kicked the giant donut-shaped sign from a donut shop at her. She dodged it, but it flew straight toward a few shrews crossing the street!

Judy raced to the rescue. Fortunately, she caught it just before it crushed one of the tiny shrews who were out shopping.

Meanwhile, Duke was about to sneak away, when—*THOOSH!*

Judy slammed the big donut sign on top of the crook . . . and made her first arrest. She took him back to ZPD Headquarters, proud of herself for her very first chase.

"I popped the weasel!" she said when she arrived back at the department.

That's how Judy became the first little bunny to handle big police work in the Zootopia Police Department. Her dream had come true!

Disney
MINNIE

The Missing Daffodils

One spring day, Daisy Duck went to her friend Minnie's house to help in the garden. But when the two got outside, they found a big surprise.

"My daffodils!" Minnie shrieked. "They're gone! I don't understand. They were here yesterday!"

"This is terrible," Daisy said. "It must be a flower prowler!"

Minnie and Daisy searched the garden for clues.

"What's this?" Daisy asked. She pulled a few fuzzy white strands off a bush near the daffodil patch.

"Maybe the flower prowler left it," Minnie said.

"Maybe," Daisy said. "Or it could be some of Figaro's hair."

A moment later, Minnie's doorbell rang. Mickey Mouse was standing on the porch with a big bunch of daffodils! Tied around them was a fluffy white ribbon.

"Oh, Mickey!" Minnie cried. "How could you? You cut down my daffodils!"

Mickey looked confused. "What do you mean, Minnie?" he asked. "I bought these at the flower shop because I know you love daffodils!"

"Really?" Minnie said, putting the flowers in a vase. She was glad that Mickey wasn't the flower prowler.

Minnie, Daisy, and Mickey decided to look around town for the flower prowler. They headed to the park and found Goofy. He was wearing a big daffodil on his vest. And he was playing with a yo-yo that had a fuzzy white string!

"Hiya, Minnie!" Goofy called. "Do you like my flower? Mr. Power is having a sale on daffodils today!"

"Hmmm . . ." said Minnie. "That's quite a coincidence."

"Maybe we'd better check out the flower shop," Daisy said.

The four friends went to Power's Flowers and peeked through the window.

"That's Mr. Power," Mickey said.

Minnie saw that the shopkeeper had a sharp pair of scissors and a fuzzy white mustache. And his shop was full of daffodils!

"He did it!" she cried. "I know it!"

Minnie and her friends burst into the shop. "Where did you get these daffodils?" Minnie asked.

"From a farmer named Mrs. Pote," Mr. Power answered. "She delivers daffodils here every day. But today she brought dozens of extras!"

Mr. Power pointed the way to Mrs. Pote's farm. "You can't miss her," he said. "She has fuzzy white hair."

Mrs. Pote's farm was called Pote's Goats.

"Yes, I delivered extra daffodils today," Mrs. Pote told Minnie. "My favorite goat, Flower, usually eats a lot of them as soon as they bloom. But she must not have been very hungry today."

That gave Minnie an idea. "May I see Flower?" she asked.

"Of course, dear," Mrs. Pote said. She led the friends to a pen. But there was no goat inside!

"Oh, my!" Mrs. Pote cried. "She must have escaped! Wherever could she have gone?"

"Look! There's a hole in the fence," Mickey said, pointing.

"Now what do we do?" Daisy exclaimed. "Not only are Minnie's daffodils gone, but so is Mrs. Pote's goat!"

"Hmmm . . ." said Minnie, deep in thought. "Maybe these two mysteries are connected!"

"What do you mean, Minnie?" Daisy asked.

"I have an idea who the flower prowler might be," Minnie explained. "It's someone who really likes daffodils. Someone who likes them even more than we do!"

Daisy held up the fuzzy strands of hair. "Don't forget this," she reminded Minnie. "Isn't it still a clue?"

"It sure is," Minnie agreed. "And so is this!" She pointed toward a trail of footprints. "Follow me!"

Minnie and the others followed the footprints straight to Daisy's yard. There was Flower, happily munching away on Daisy's flowers.

"See?" Minnie said. "I knew it! There's our flower prowler. Now if we could only train her to like weeds instead!"

INCREDIBLES 2

A Day Out with Mom

Helen was happy to be back with her family. Hero work had taken her away for a long time, and she missed spending time with her family.

She knew Bob was still a little worn out from taking care of everything in her absence, so she had an idea. "Why don't you go do something fun today?" she suggested.

Bob sprang up and kissed Helen on the cheek. "Thanks, honey! See you guys later!" he called.

After breakfast, Helen had another great idea. "Hey, Violet. Why don't you come with me to drop Dash off at track practice, and then we can go shopping for your first date with Tony?"

"I don't know . . ." said Violet.

"Come on," said Helen. "It'll be mother-daughter fun!"

Helen and the kids piled into the car and headed out. When they arrived at Dash's school, they found an empty parking lot. "Oh, no. I forgot practice is canceled today!" Dash said.

"Well, you can help with Jack-Jack," said Helen. "Then Vi and I can focus on shopping."

"Great . . . babysitting," said Dash.

Dash zoomed around the mall with Jack-Jack in the stroller.

"Dash!" Helen yelled. "No running with the baby!"

Dash knew he wasn't supposed to use his powers in public for fun.

"I'm battling the evils of boredom," he explained.

Helen raised her eyebrows and said, "Stop."

Helen and Violet began picking out things for Violet to try on, but Dash and Jack-Jack kept distracting them.

"Here," Helen said, handing Dash some cash and forcing a smile. "Take your brother on the carousel and go enjoy the mall. Meet us at the fountain in an hour."

"Thanks!" said Dash.

Helen sighed. "Okay. Now we can focus."

Violet tried on some dresses, but none of them seemed right.

They went into another shop, and Violet found an outfit she liked. "This is cute," she said.

"But so casual," said Helen. She held up a couple of dresses. "Look at these!"

Violet smiled weakly and took them into the dressing room.

Meanwhile, Dash and Jack-Jack were having a blast! They rode on the carousel and bought lots and lots of candy.

"Now this is living," said Dash as he and Jack-Jack enjoyed their sweets in a train car.

At the end of the hour, Violet sat with Helen, feeling a little sad that they hadn't found anything.

As Dash and Jack-Jack raced up to the fountain, Helen frowned.

"Sorry we're late," blurted Dash, showing off a colorful smile.

Before Helen could say a word, an alarm blared! A woman from the jewelry store shouted, "Thief!"

The family slapped on their masks and revealed their Supersuits. They darted into the jewelry store, but the thief was gone.

"He appeared out of nowhere," said the clerk. "He took the jewelry and vanished."

Elastigirl and the kids scanned the store, looking for clues.

Suddenly, another store alarm blared! The family took off toward it.

A chorus of alarms rang from every corner of the mall!

"Maybe it's a team of thieves," said Elastigirl.

"Or maybe he can multiply, like Jack-Jack," said Violet. Hearing that, Jack-Jack multiplied, and each baby wandered off in a different direction.

Violet and Elastigirl collected as many Jack-Jacks as they could while Dash raced off to find the thief.

Dash spotted the burglar and could tell right away: he was definitely a Supervillain. As Dash rushed toward him, he vanished in a flash of light.

Dash didn't notice the burglar reappear right behind him.

Elastigirl entered and tried to stretch-grab the villain, but he disappeared and reappeared at a register behind her!

"Name's Blindspot," he said, disappearing again.

All the Jack-Jacks in Elastigirl's arms merged back into one, and together, Jack-Jack, Violet, Dash, and Elastigirl went after the thief.

Violet scooped up Jack-Jack and cued him to use his laser eyes. But Blindspot disappeared again!

Even with Dash's super speed, he wasn't fast enough to catch the vanishing villain.

Elastigirl created a labyrinth of traps, hoping to trip him up. But Blindspot managed to disappear and reappear his way through the mall.

Then Violet caught Blindspot's reflection in a mirror and realized something: he was traveling through their blind spots! She quickly used a compact mirror to spot him, then threw a force field to trap him inside. The entire family ran alongside the Supervillain as he rolled through the mall.

Just then, a dress in a shop window caught Elastigirl's attention. "Vi! That'd look great on you!"

"Mom," said Violet, "I don't want to disappoint you, but . . . I don't really like dresses."

"I'm sorry, Vi," said Elastigirl. "I just wanted to spend some quality time with you."

Elastigirl anchored the force field to the fountain, locking the trapped Blindspot in place.

"Well, you got your wish," said Violet, smiling. "Nothing says family bonding like catching a Supervillain together!"

As the family headed out, Helen turned to Violet. "You know . . . I have no idea what I wore on my first date with your father. Clothes don't really matter. Wear something you like."

Later that week, Violet put on her favorite jeans and T-shirt and went downstairs.

"You look beautiful," said Helen.

"Thanks, Mom," said Violet, giving her mother a big hug. She was ready for her first date with Tony!

Tiana's Big-City Sound

One beautiful fall day in New Orleans, Tiana received a letter. Her cousin Freda was the leader of a band in New York City, and she had invited Tiana to a show!

Tiana had never been to New York before. She couldn't wait to hear her cousin's band play.

Tiana left Naveen in charge of her restaurant, Tiana's Palace, and boarded a train heading north.

Tiana settled into her seat and got ready for a long ride. But the train was so much fun, she hardly noticed the hours going by. Tiana loved watching the countryside from her train car window.

But none of the sights were as impressive as the New York City skyline. The skyscrapers of the tiny island towered over the sparkling river.

When Tiana came out of the train station, she couldn't believe how many people were there. She was surrounded by flashing lights. And everywhere she looked she saw screeching streetcars and racing taxis.

Tiana couldn't wait to see her cousin. She took out Freda's letter and read that she had to get to Harlem. A stranger pointed toward the subway. Tiana rode all the way to Harlem, lulled by the sounds of the big city.

When Tiana arrived at the theater, her cousin came running out to greet her.

Freda was just as Tiana remembered—full of energy.

"I'm so glad you're here," Freda said, pulling Tiana into a big hug. "But I have some bad news. Our usual joint is closing." Freda explained there wouldn't be any show.

"No show?" Tiana exclaimed. "But surely you can find somewhere else to play."

She wanted to help. Tiana promised Freda and the band she would find them a new venue for their show.

Tiana and the band tried theater after theater, club after club. No one was willing to take a chance on Freda's band.

"Let's face it, Freda," the saxophonist said. "We're out of luck."

"I guess I'll go back to working at my uncle's diner," the guitarist added. "Playing in a band was just a silly dream."

"No!" Tiana said. "We can't give up! Not yet!"

Just then, it started raining. Freda and the band put their instruments over their heads and raced toward the large library across the street.

"Thanks for all your help, Tiana," Freda whispered as she and her cousin dried their feet.

Tiana wished she knew what to do. She looked up at the high window, hoping to catch a glimpse of Evangeline, the Evening Star. Back home, whenever Tiana didn't know what to do, she would make a wish on the big bright star.

Tiana couldn't see Evangeline. But she could see the high ceilings of the library's main room. She could see the lovely old windows and the neatly arranged tables and chairs. It reminded her of her restaurant. Suddenly, she had an idea.

Tiana grabbed a pen and paper and started making plans. Then she talked to the librarians.

When the head librarian heard Tiana's idea, she called her colleagues over.

"We've been talking about hosting some cultural nights," she said. "This might be the perfect way to get started!"

Tiana introduced Freda to the librarians. Together, they started planning.

That night, long after the library would normally close, it was full
of people. When Freda and her band started playing, even more folks
crowded in. They wanted to know who was making such amazing music.
Tiana wasn't surprised. Her cousin's band really was the bee's knees.

After the show, bookers crowded around Freda, competing to get her band to play at their theaters. Everyone else crowded around the librarians, asking what they would see at the library next.

Tiana watched from the library doorway. Her plan had worked—even better than she could have dreamed.

Later, when all the people had gone home, Tiana and Freda went to a deli for a late-night snack.

"Thanks for your help," Freda said. "We never would have played the library without it."

"I have an idea for your next venue, too," Tiana said. "Tiana's Palace—it's the bee's knees!"